Previou

Praise for The Tabat Quartet books

"A fascinating world of magic, intrigue, and revolution . . . a promising start to a distinctive fantasy series."
—PUBLISHERS WEEKLY

"A beautifully written book, lyrical and poetic, and it lingers in the mind long after the last page is turned."
—YSABEAU WILCE, author of the Flora Trilogy

"This novel dares to be different and offers excellent entertainment to readers who want to read good and thought-provoking stories . . . An excellent fantasy."
—RISING SHADOW

"[A] lush tapestry of a story."
—FANTASY LITERATURE

Praise for Near + Far

"Wonderful in its sheer variety . . . Her prose is smooth as a dream but often hides an incredibly sharp, emotive edge."
—TOR.COM

"Rambo's range is galaxy-wide: she goes from near-future quasi-dystopia to far-future space opera, from slapstick humor to Eurypidean tragedy, with deceptively effortless prose, like a prima ballerina executing grandes jetés."
—SF SIGNAL

ALSO BY CAT RAMBO

NOVELS

Beasts of Tabat
Hearts of Tabat

COLLECTIONS

Altered America
Near + Far
Neither Here Nor There
Eyes Like Sky and Coal and Moonlight
The Surgeon's Tale and Other Stories (with Jeff VanderMeer)

CARPE GLITTER

a novelette by

CAT RAMBO

Meerkat Press
Atlanta

ISBN-13 978-1-946154-53-8 (Paperback)
ISBN-13 978-1-946154-34-7 (eBook)

Library of Congress Control Number: 2019951065

Cover Art by Zoomfish Studio

Printed in the United States of America

Published in the United States of America by
Meerkat Press, LLC, Atlanta, Georgia
www.meerkatpress.com

For Wayne, Always.

Carpe glitter, my grandmother Gloria always said. Seize the glitter.

And that was what I remembered best about her, the glitter: a dazzle of rhinestone, a waft of Patou Joy, lipstick like a red banner across her mouth. Underneath all that, a wiry little old lady with silver hair and vampire-pale skin.

Not that she was a vampire, of course. But Gloria Aim hung with everyone who was anyone during her days in the Vegas crowd. Celebrities, presidents, journalists, they all came to her show at the Sparkle Dome, watched her strut her stuff in a black top hat and fishnet stockings, conjuring flames and doves (never card tricks, which she hated), making ghosts speak to loved ones in the audience. And when she stepped off the stage, she left in a scintillating dazzle, like a fairy queen stepping off her throne.

All that shine. And at home?

She was a grubby hoarder.

I mopped sweat off my forehead with the hem of my T-shirt and attacked another pile of magazines. Dust wafted up to fill my nostrils and make me sneeze, drifted down to coat the hairs on my forearms with grit. Something had rotted in the corner; I was doing that side once I'd cleared a path to it and breathing through my mouth in the meantime.

This had once been intended as a guest room, but it had been taken over by a troupe of china-headed dolls, stacked atop piles of brittle newspapers and magazines. No cat pee—I'd been spared that in these back rooms, closed off for at least a couple of decades.

Grandmother had bought the house when she was at the height of her first fortune. She'd just burst onto the stage magician scene, a woman from Brooklyn who'd trained herself in sleight of hand and studied under the most famous female stage magician of *her* time, Susan Day.

The nearest heap of magazines, in fact, flaking away at my touch, showed Grandmother and her mentor on the uppermost cover, a poster from their brief tour together, just after World War II. Glamorous older Day, blonde hair worn in a sleek chignon and eyes blue as turquoise. Grandmother bright and shiny not just from the rhinestones glittering across her chest, but starry-eyed—her grin so wide it stretched her mouth.

The stack held dozens of copies of the same issue, no matter how far down I went. A swarm of silverfish scurried away as I lifted the last one. I'd get the room cleared before bringing out my arsenal of bug spray for an onslaught.

Yellowed confetti bits fell away as I put the stack on the heap to be bagged up and trashed. By now I'd learned that paper flaking that badly meant the appraiser's regretful headshake and the murmur, "Too badly eroded, Miss Aim."

As with each of the seven rooms I'd managed so far, I sorted the contents into piles. *Throw away* was by far the largest. *To be appraised* had interesting things in it beyond the scads of dolls Grandmother had collected. *Keep* was actually two subpiles, one for Mother and one for me.

Object after object to be evaluated and sorted. Old magazines and flutters of candy wrappers. So much clothing, most of it absurdly formal, scratchy with ancient starch. Theater props piled on top of grab bags she'd picked up at church rummage sales, still unopened. Half-filled perfume bottles and compacts full of sweet dust.

And then there were oddities: a picture stitched of human hair, showing a castle on a cliff; an enormous crystal ball, a good foot and a half wide; a mechanical banjo trio that played itself, complete with a library of antebellum songs to choose from; a basket stuffed with sandalwood fans.

The "rotting thing" turned out to be a heap of furs that, when stirred, sent up a stench reminiscent of old sauerkraut that sent me out into the hallway for a while to lean against the yellowing wallpaper and breathe in fresher air.

The doll collection was worth a good bit, perhaps, I'd been told. But nothing on the scale of financial windfall I had hoped for. Grandmother had been wealthy, even though she kept her spending discreet, aside from this strange mishmash of a house. Where had all that money gone?

And why had she saved everything? I thought that it was perhaps a return to her childhood days, which had been uncertain and full of moves. My great-grandfather had been a con man, always on the edge of getting run out of town, according to her stories. They'd had to leave in the middle of the night more than once, abandoning anything that couldn't go into a suitcase. This could be a reaction to that.

There was no point psychoanalyzing my dead grandmother, though. Once the furs were bagged up and taken out, the room was much more bearable. I kept on searching, working through the last of the piles before examining the desiccated rug underneath, so dry I was worried it might crumble away if I tried to vacuum it.

My cell vibrated against my hip. I slid it out of my shorts pocket and glanced at the screen. My mother.

I took a breath before thumbing the phone on. "Yes?" I said.

"I wish you hadn't chosen this," Mother said, launching

right back into the same argument we'd been having all week, ever since I'd said, "Actually, I'll take the second option" at the reading of the will. "It's ridiculous. You could probably tell them that you've changed your mind, that you want the money instead."

"You never know, I might turn up something wonderful," I said, trying a new tack. Maybe if I could convince her that there might be treasure buried in the piles and heaps lining this massive amalgamation of three houses, she'd support me in this.

She hissed impatience. At least that's what that strangled sound had always meant for both her and Grandmother. Mother liked to pretend she was Grandmother's antithesis, but the truth was, they were more alike than either would have admitted. I had even found a mannerism or two I didn't think of as mine, but *theirs*, creeping into my own speech. *"Have* you found anything?" she demanded.

"Not yet," I said. "But I've only begun to scratch the surface. You have no idea how much stuff she managed to cram into this place. It's a little mind-blowing." I toed at the pile I'd been sorting, and it slid sideways with a waft of cedar and old socks that almost made me gag.

"Why are you being so stubborn about this, Persephone?"

"I'm thirty years old. I get to make my own choices. Grandmother offered them to me." I hesitated before adding, "It's not your call," feeling the words slide distance between us when my mother was already so far away.

She hung up without a word. I stared at "Connection terminated" before wiping at my face again, tasting salt on my lips. I was sweating up a storm in this fierce heat. That's all it was.

⌣

When I graduated from high school and Grandmother said she wouldn't pay for college, I pleaded with my mother to intercede. "*You caused this,*" I said. "I'm not asking you to tell me what happened. It's all between you and her. I'm not taking sides. But if you went to her . . ."

Mother shook her head quickly, nervously shaking away any chance. Her hands, long fingered and dexterous as my grandmother's, as my own, twisted in front of her, as though signing negation.

I put my arm down on the kitchen table, and immediately regretted it. We were living in an apartment over a diner; it always smelled of old hamburgers, and every surface acquired a sticky, oily film that felt like cling wrap sticking to the skin. Next door, one of the three Laotian women that lived there began yelling at another in one of their interminable arguments.

"No, no," my mother said, words tumbling, desperation driven. Just the mention of Grandmother sent her into a panic. "Let's not talk about that. But think of what else you can do. You wrote all those wonderful essays for the literary magazine. Surely they must have some scholarship fund for promising students. Or if you join the National Guard, they'll pay, and then you'd know what you were doing, straight out of college!"

"Mom." I shook my head, mirroring her gesture in slow motion. "Do you think I didn't look into every other option? The time for applying for scholarships is long past. I'd have to postpone school for a year—"

"Then postpone it for a year! You can live here, find a job, put money aside—"

"No!" I'd seen too many other people let a year turn into two, then three. Then never. There's always something to eat away whatever funds you have.

I had to grab the chance while I could. I'd watched the

meager wage my mother made as a secretary in the years since my grandmother stopped subsidizing us melt away every month. Always something—a roof to be fixed, my mother's ulcer operation, a thousand car problems.

I'd stepped up and managed all that, getting part-time jobs, but never enough. Never money to put away for college. And I hadn't thought about that, always assuming my grandmother would pay my way. I didn't expect to live lavishly—I was more than willing to keep working—but without her funds, I was sunk.

I could have cried then, but what good would that have done, other than tying my mother up in knots?

So I went to see my grandmother.

Her place was the same as always: a compound of sorts, made up of three houses grown together. No grass lawn, but an elaborate landscape of cacti and other desert plants: huge striped agave and overgrown saguaro that Grandmother had a gardener put in before I was born, long before anyone used terms like "xeriscaping" or "drought-tolerant."

Two of the houses had started out as single-level, only to gain rooftop decks, gazebos, and a shed-piled-on-shed construction that would have never survived in an area with actual weather. The third and last to be added to the mélange was a three-story Tudor, on the northern side. I came in through the entrance of the first house, which was where Grandmother kept most of the rooms that she used from day to day.

I knew about the hoarding. I'd spent plenty of summer afternoons in my childhood playing in the vast complex, given free rein by my grandmother, who would shoo me off

in order to settle in for an afternoon of practicing prestidig-
itation or designing trick cabinets in her large workshop,
which filled a three-car garage and was where I'd built my
first birdhouse, bookcase, and tiny wooden box.

The front door, set with a fan of red and gold stained
glass, resounded under my knock. Once I would have just
let myself in. I still had a key somewhere, but she'd always
changed the locks on a yearly basis, although she'd never
explain why. Beyond that, every lock had its own individual
key, so you had to know which one yours fit.

Inside, though, few doors held locks, other than the door to
Grandmother's inner sanctum, a book-lined study surround-
ing an enormous ebony and mother-of-pearl desk littered
with diagrams and correspondence. Only Grandmother and
her secretaries held *that* key—perhaps the motivation for the
yearly lock change, although you would have thought that
it only would have happened when one of them left if that
were the case.

I used the knocker, an elaborate bronze cast of two Chinese
dragons. Grandmother loved mysticism and loaded her act
with as many symbols of it as she could. Many of her fans
came repeatedly to shows, trying to decipher the potpourri
of cabalistic and arcane clues she managed to incorporate
into her costumes and equipment.

The door swung open with a waft of musky incense. I'd
expected a secretary, but it was Grandmother herself. She'd
shrunk; where once she'd reached my ear, she was closer
to shoulder high, but still carried herself like the lead flag
bearer in a parade.

"Come in," she said, as though she'd seen me only the
day before. She turned and walked away, clearly expecting
me to follow her.

I did, stepping into the reception area that was one of my

favorite rooms. The enormous bay window showed a view of the cactus garden outside, refracted and split a thousand different ways by the curtain of crystals strung on translucent fishing line. The furniture's well-worn cobalt velvet presented a silky shimmer in the weave, neon electric minnows scattering across ocean surface. This was where Grandmother often received visitors, not allowing them to enter any deeper into the house.

I didn't remember it being this crammed, however, stuffed to the point of claustrophobia. The walls were lined with shelves that reached above my head, lined in turn with an array of dolls, ranging in size from tiny to knee-high, dressed in elaborate costumes. I recognized some, dressed to mirror stage costumes Grandmother had worn over the years; I'd played with the originals more than once.

Other dolls stood on the mantelpiece, in a few other odd corners, or lined the windowsills. Some had been placed along the wall, standing, in a long line.

In the corner, boxes were stacked, labels reading "Limited Edition" followed by my grandmother's name, inset windows showing the dolls inside. The air smelled of horsehair and dust and aging plastic.

The table—placed knee-bump close between two chairs—held a silver tray with coffee pot, cups, cream and sugar, a small plate of cookies, and two cloth napkins. Had Grandmother been expecting me? I couldn't imagine that my mother would have called ahead to warn her.

I settled into the chair across from her and picked up a cookie as she poured for both of us. Saying nothing, she fixed the cup just the way I liked it—a splash of milk, half a spoonful of sugar—while I nibbled at the edge of the cookie, which tasted like cardboard and lemon.

Without preamble, she said, "You're here because you need money for college."

"Not a lot," I said. "I plan on working to cover my food and housing, and going in-state will keep the cost down."

"I'm prepared to pay your full tuition and living expenses under specific conditions," she said.

I blinked. "Which are?"

She set down her own cup in order to tick them off on two fingers. "A. You will attend the university of my choice. B. You will major in the field of my choice."

"What?" I said. Something between indignation and panic swept through me, made me lean forward. "What university? What major?" Who knew what sort of weirdness she'd arrived at?

"You can go out of state," she said. "But it must be on the East Coast. Preferably MIT."

"Why MIT?"

"That's where Susan Day went. My tribute to her."

"What was her major?"

"That part doesn't come into play. I want you to study engineering."

"What?" My forehead crinkled in puzzlement. "Why engineering?"

"I didn't say I would explain any of it," she said, and picked up her cup to take another sip.

I had no leverage, no bargaining power. I agreed to every term she laid out. When I told my mother that I'd be going to MIT, she didn't ask where the money was coming from or why I'd picked it.

Don't ask, don't tell. So I said nothing.

Imagine all the detritus a person creates during a lifetime. I'm not talking about trash—food wrappers and old boxes—but objects that we interact with, that we make: grocery lists and summer postcards, books we scrawl notes in during school, journals and letters and drawings.

And photographs. God, the photographs!

Grandmother was a celebrity and celebrities are documented, in slides and old Polaroids and dusty rolls of film. Newspaper clippings and the pinup poses autographed and sent to fans by one of the series of blond male secretaries handling Grandmother's correspondence, invisible as house sparrows. None of them lasted more than a couple of years; none had been mentioned in Grandmother's will. Much like my mother.

All contained in cardboard boxes with tape gone age-brittle, crumbling when touched. At least the Las Vegas heat and dryness had spared me mold, and insects other than the endless silverfish and occasional scorpion, and somehow, amazingly, it appeared no mouse had ever ventured within these walls. Grandmother must have put down poison for them, or else a secretary had intervened at some point.

I progressed, box by slow box. I picked up the pace as I went, learning to sort better, or perhaps just caring less in the face of this bewildering mass of *stuff*.

Often I found things that seemed to have been packed by mistake. A roll of paper towels, a willowware bowl full of ancient crackers gone gray as cardboard. A rake swaddled in a blanket. Half a dozen flowerpots, a packet of marigold seeds from 1963, unused gardening gloves and a tiny, dollhouse-sized shovel. Glass ashtrays with cigarette butts and the crumpled ends of joints mingled with the ash. A cracked jar of shea butter. Old Halloween masks and classroom valentines from Grandmother's childhood, signed in straggling pencil:

Ursula, Jimmy, Laverne. Taxidermied animals, including a panda, an iguana, and a goat with a unicorn horn grafted on.

I hoped for treasure. And I did find a few pieces to set aside, here and there, but too often it was trash. Grandmother's jewelry boxes glittered promise when I opened the lid and let the light in, but all that sparkle was an illusion. Good costume jewelry, the appraiser told me, and not entirely worthless because it was vintage. But far from the dragon's hoard I'd first thought it to be. How could anything so glittery be worth so little?

The strangest thing I found that first week was a metal hand. Fully articulated and as finely fingered as my own hand, splayed beside it for comparison, although the metal one was larger than mine by half. It wasn't gold, but it resembled it. And old—it felt decades old. The engraving on it was so fine that I couldn't make it out at first.

When I squinted at it, holding it in a sunbeam coming in through the window, I saw it was swastikas and lightning bolts, an interlocking pattern. Graceful in its design, but I had the same reaction to it that war and other atrocities always evoked, a twist of nausea at the pit of my stomach.

Some war souvenir Day had collected? The hand had a scientific feel to it, and I remembered that Day had spied on German scientists, infiltrated them, pretending to be a Nazi sympathizer. Perhaps it was a working model, a prototype of some sort, rather than art object?

The stump was sealed off with a metal cap set with fine, deep grooves. It felt odd in my grip. Loose, as though its center of gravity kept changing. And as though it might move at any moment, might twitch itself from my hands and do some strange and sinister thing (it was indeed a left hand).

What had my grandmother done with it? Or had she done anything? So many of the objects here were unused, still in their original wrappings. So perhaps she hadn't used it at all. Any answer would probably lie in my grandmother's bedroom suite, which I hadn't dared tackle yet. Those rooms might have seemed ample in my childhood, but now they were crammed, a maze of twisty little passages defined by cartons and shoeboxes, round hat and wig boxes, tiny vanity tables heaped with cosmetics in wholesale quantities.

I had cleared a room my first day, one of the downstairs guest bedrooms, through the simple expedient of stacking its contents wherever else I could, including a bunch of plastic tubs out in the courtyard. Instinct, perhaps, or a premonition that I'd need that space.

Despite the yellowing wallpaper, the dust ground into the ancient hardwood floor, and the same smell of incense that permeated the first few rooms, it was an orderly place where I could retreat when overwhelmed by the chaos. I kept it scrupulously clean so it might feel like a refuge—free of loose dust and smelling faintly of lemon, the bed made with the sky-blue silk comforter embroidered with golden stars and crimson butterflies, taken from an upstairs bedroom, that I'd always loved, always coveted. My suitcase sat on a rack, empty, all of its contents transferred to the closet's six hangers and the tiny dresser's three drawers.

There was a washer and dryer in the basement, so I didn't fear going without clean clothes. Ever since my college years, I'd grown used to living out of a backpack, resisting the nesting urge that seemed to claim all the other women of my family.

No other adornments in the room: no art, no rug, no knickknacks or votive candles. I took the hand and put it on the dresser.

It was late and I was tired. But whenever I closed my eyes, I couldn't help but imagine that hand, lifting itself on its fingertips, crawling silently down the side of the dresser, creeping toward me. Finally I got up and put it in the bottom dresser drawer, which was otherwise empty, and closed it tightly. The old wood was sticky—if the hand tried to escape, it would make enough noise to wake me.

With that thought, I was finally able to sleep.

⌒

I can tell you exactly when Grandmother started hoarding. My mother had told me the story. Grandmother started collecting the dolls when she was a girl, but at least the collection had been manageable. Things wouldn't reach the untenable stage until after I was an adolescent.

When Susan Day died, she'd named Grandmother as her only heir, so Grandmother'd had the contents of Day's Brooklyn brownstone, a large pre-war place, shipped to her home in Vegas. At the same time, she bought the house next door and had a breezeway installed to link them. The old occupant's furniture was left in place and combined with the new—creating an unholy amalgamation of seventies avocado and toasted almond decor mixed with Old-World German wood carvings, cabalistic statues and seventy Chinese urns (I counted them once).

I remember visiting that doubled house. Even then it was cramped and odd, but when you're a child everything is normal.

When I was thirteen, there was a neighbor girl, Elena. We played together outside. I don't think I consciously tried to keep her out of the house, but I didn't volunteer to take her in. She pushed for it, and I ended up agreeing on a sleepover.

I didn't think much about her motives. I was tentatively thrilled to have a girl my age who wanted to be friends. My mother and I had moved so often that I hadn't experienced it much. And my grandmother wisely stayed out of the way, aside from ordering us a pizza, telling us to behave, and vanishing into her workshop for the rest of the evening.

My room had twin beds, so we each took one. Long after "bedtime," we lay there, talking about school and what classes we hated.

"Man, everyone's going to flip that I spent the night here," Elena said.

"Why?" Uneasiness wriggled through me at her tone.

"Nobody else has ever been in here. People who try to sell magazines, candy, whatever fundraising bullshit the school has given you, your grandmother doesn't even open the door. They call it the witch house."

I forced a laugh. "Well, now you can tell them it's not a witch house."

There was some silence before Elena said, "Yeah, now I can tell them."

In the morning, we went into the big kitchen that Grandmother used. The one in the other house was small and cramped: she referred to it as "the party kitchen" despite the fact that she never, in all the time I knew her, held a party there.

I opened the cupboard and showed Elena the breakfast cereal choices. I always ate the sugarcoated cereal my mother wouldn't permit me at home, and Grandmother was good about getting it stocked up before my visit.

Elena opted for something more adult, although she did reach for the sugar bowl as I handed her the corn flakes.

"Oh, *gross*," she said.

She'd upended the cereal box over her bowl and what emerged was a mix of flakes, tiny brown bugs, and even tinier white grubs.

Every box in the cupboard other than my presweetened stuff was like that, I found out when I went back later. Elena gave up after the third try and went home. We never talked to each other again; I saw her duck away a few times when our paths would have crossed.

A few years later, Grandmother bought the house in back and did the same thing, joining it, but this time, built actual hallways. In the center, the enclosed courtyard held a gargantuan pool, in which I floated away innumerable summer afternoons, and a neglected rock garden, overgrown with sedum and hen and chicks plants which sprouted everywhere they could seize hold. I have never seen that variety elsewhere. They'd originally appeared in nine purple planters, but had spread throughout the garden, ousting the more ordinary varieties in the process.

The plants had an odd purplish hue and bore clusters of white flowers that opened only at sunset, filling the courtyard with an ineffable, sweet smell that to me will always be the smell of homesickness.

⌒

I woke smelling that wonderful smell, wafting in through the open window. At first, I didn't know what had broken my sleep, but it came again: a knock at the door. So I went to the door and opened it.

"Ms. Aim?" the first man said. He pronounced it with the faintest of Southern accents: Miz Ay-yum. It was a young voice, but the man didn't match. The gray of his suit washed out his skin to a pallid hue and turned his crew cut hair the same muddy color. The man standing a little behind him was shorter, squatter, darker, but had the same unremarkable sit and general appearance. "We understand you're sorting through your grandmother's estate and we had some questions."

"I'd like to see some identification," I said.

"Of course." He held out a card.

"Anyone can forge something like this," I said, turning over the stiff plastic. It was well-worn, at least. "I've never heard of this agency, Mr. Forest. The Department of War History?"

Agent Alan Forest flashed a tight smile. "All we'd like to do is talk to you, Ms. Aim. Preferably not here on the street."

My estimation of him went up a notch when he didn't bat an eyelash at the decor as he stepped inside.

His partner, though, made a small choked sound as he looked around. "You're wading through all this?" he said. "Man, I don't envy you. My great-aunt, she was a hoarder too. Three years now and we're still turning up storage lockers where she stashed stuff."

He sounded genuine, but the first man stepped in to follow up too smoothly. "We're prepared to offer help with the task, Ms. Aim. A crew of professional appraisers to sort through the place and prepare an inventory, suggest where to dispose of everything. No charge to you."

"But you want something of hers in exchange."

"We have reason to believe she may have some items of historical interest, inherited from Ms. Day. While your grandmother was alive, we approached her repeatedly, but she expressed reluctance to go through everything she'd acquired from Ms. Day. She indicated it'd be taken care of in the will, but apparently she never got around to including that clause."

His tone pressed all the right keys. I felt apologetic—I knew how stubborn she could be. I actually stepped forward, ready to agree to whatever he wanted. But a glint of sunlight danced through one of the crystals hanging in the big bay window and dazzled my eyes for a second, just long enough for me to catch my breath and shut my mouth so hard and quick that my teeth clicked together.

"I'm sorry," I said. Expectation lit his eyes, only to be extinguished the next second when I continued: "I'll need to think this over."

They both insisted on leaving their cards. I threw them on a heap in the room where I was sticking recyclables until the city could send a truck next week. I'd learned the hard way that garbage is something city officials take very seriously and that placing enough bags to fill an entire truck on a curbside may lead to you having to take the majority of those bags back inside, or at least as far as an enclosed porch.

The will's phrasing had made me think Grandmother had wanted me to take the house. To sort through her belongings, to understand the life they represented? But I had to wonder if she'd realized how awful it would be.

What was this house, if not a monument to held regrets? Glitter takes movement. By clutching it so hard, stuffing it into boxes, she'd taken away everything she loved about it.

I shook out an ancient stage gown. Sequins fell away like fish scales, whisper-sifting onto the floor at my feet. All that was left was a skeleton of bone and ancient tulle that stood upright for a second, as though a ghost were wearing it, before it crumpled to the floor.

∁

My grandmother knew plenty of other stage magicians. Of them all, my favorite was Eterno. That was why, when I bumped into him at the grocery store that afternoon, I was so delighted that I hugged him. He hugged back, an avuncular, almost paternal, pressure. He was a large man, a square face all beard and moustache, snowy as a mountain now. He was dressed formally—he had always insisted on that—and his tie-clip was a pair of silver masks, one laughing, one weeping.

"What are you doing here? I asked as we steered our carts together toward the checkout line.

"I was visiting a friend in the area, figured I'd stop on my way home, pick up lunch. Build my strength back up." He winked.

I wrinkled my nose at him. "I don't need to know the details of your sex life, thank you very much."

He roared with laughter. "Think the oldsters don't get it on, my girl? How wrong you are. Oh, how very wrong you are."

I put my hands over my ears. "La-la-la-la-la, I can't hear you."

"Come and get coffee, child."

We settled into the leather armchairs of the generic coffee shop attached to the grocery.

Eterno had ordered some sort of lavish coffee and accoutrements drink; he eyed my drip coffee with amusement. "You were always such a purist as a child; I shouldn't be surprised. How is the great purge going?"

"So much stuff, I said. "A bunch of pictures of you I set aside. You guys look so happy together. Were you and Grandmother ever . . . you know . . ." I made a little gesture with my hand but I'm not sure what exactly it was supposed to convey.

He stared at me. "Of course we were. How can you ask that?"

"I was a child," I said. "I didn't know."

He picked up his elaborate drink and sipped from it, eyes never leaving mine. "You never wondered?"

"Wondered if you were involved? Sure."

Hair fell to obscure his eyes as he shook his head. "I mean, whether I was really your grandfather or not."

"Are you?"

He sipped. "Let me say it's a definite possibility. Maybe even a probability."

"Can we get a DNA test?"

His eyebrow lifted. "You were always such a pragmatic child as well. But no."

"Why not?"

"Because your grandmother never saw fit to. That was her choice. Who am I to contravene that?" He spread his long-fingered conjurer's hands in a helpless gesture.

I stared at him. "If you really were my grandfather, you'd have every right to tell me," I said, "Ergo, you are not." I felt a little sad for the possibility, even as logic banished it.

He sighed. He leaned forward. "Listen, kiddo, I'm on your side no matter what. Have you found anything strange while going through her things?"

My mind flashed on the metal hand, but I kept my face blank—no one plays poker like a conjurer's kid—and said, "What sort of strange things?"

"She bought a lot of magic memorabilia over the years," he said. "Some of it is cursed. Take it out of whatever protection surrounds it and you might trigger all sorts of unwanted side effects."

I scoffed. "You're acting like all of this is real."

He just looked at me, scorn twisting his lips.

We both knew that it was real.

We'd both seen her do things that only magic could have done.

∽

The leg startled me when I found it. It wasn't that I was surprised to find a leg, just that I had thought it would manifest in small bits: shin, knee, thigh. Instead it was all one piece; quite heavy, although not as weighty as one might have expected, so it was clearly hollow. I could make the knee flex both backward and forward; it moved smoothly and without a trace of stiffness. Almost naturally.

I put it in the closet. How many of these would I find? A whole man's worth? Was this the ultimate doll in Grandmother's collection? Some of her "magic memorabilia"?

Was it something magical?

$$\backsim$$

When I was eight, my grandmother eclipsed the moon for me.

She did it as a trick. Eterno was over and they'd been drinking elaborate cocktails made by the current secretary. I'd said, "Will you do a trick, Nana?"

She said, in the affected drawl that took over her speech whenever she was tipsy, "I'll do a *real* trick for you."

Eterno held my hand and we both sat there in the courtyard as my grandmother moved around it, muttering to herself. She plucked her hairpins out and her white hair unwound and fell down her back—longer than I had ever suspected it of being. She cried out something to the heavens, and we saw the blackness of the sky writhe and begin to eat the moon. The light turned cold, the streetlights having extinguished themselves at some point when I hadn't noticed. I could feel Eterno's heartbeat in his fingers against mine and hear his breathing.

Somehow, I sensed he was as terrified as I was. Because this meant it was a different world than we'd suspected, one with rules that we didn't comprehend. For a child, it was not that devastating. I can't imagine what it was like for an adult.

All in all, it lasted perhaps an hour. The cold light from nowhere pierced us, and I could hear singing, a high-pitched singing that sounded like terror and giddy delight all at once. It was hard to take in air; every lungful had to be battled for.

When the blackness released the moon, we could breathe again.

But none of us ever spoke about it after that night. I got the impression that my grandmother regretted it.

A good magician never reveals their tricks.

⌇

There was nothing else to do but tackle what I'd put off for so long: Grandmother's suite. It occupied a good half of the Tudor house's second floor: bedroom, lavishly appointed bath, sitting room. The high ceilings might have been lovely but they also allowed her to stack the boxes even taller there, towering above me so high I couldn't reach the top layers of most stacks, making me wonder how my tiny grandmother had managed until I spotted the folding stepstool wedged in a corner.

I'd avoided this spot even though it made no sense. If there were valuables, this was the logical place for them. No, something else deterred me. Elsewhere in the house I could explore and pretend that my grandmother had just stepped out for a moment. To invade her bedroom, that was a different thing.

That was to acknowledge that she was dead.

I don't believe in glorifying the dead. I will not pretend that my grandmother was a nice woman. I will not pretend that she was a kind woman. In truth, she was self-absorbed, strong-minded to the point of being a force of nature.

But she loved me. I was her only grandchild and when I

was smaller, I could have done no wrong in her eyes. That was, perhaps, one of the things that had divided my mother and me. She'd tried so hard all her life for her own mother's approval while I'd gotten it without even asking.

When someone loves you like that, deeply and unconditionally, it's very hard not to love them back. My grandmother may have coerced me into the college of her choosing, but we'd both known the truth: while she'd done plenty to use me to hurt my mother in the long and complicated game they'd been playing all their lives, keeping me hostage was a strategy that would have worked for either side. My mother had not used it, but I wasn't sure if that was through unawareness or some moral scruple. I'd never understood all the currents of emotion that ran between them.

I paused in front of the oak double doors. They weren't original to the house—she'd brought them back from somewhere in Bavaria. Carved with willow trees and Rhine maidens, each boasted a handle made of a brass swan. I laid my fingers on a swan's neck and tried the handle: locked. I sighed and began testing keys from the vast loop of unmarked ones I'd found in the kitchen. After ten minutes of trial and error, the lock clicked and I swung the door open.

I found the light switch and flipped it back and forth, but the bulb was burned out. You couldn't see the room for all the boxes, blocking most of the light from the windows. A narrow passageway led between the stacks of cardboard cartons—some old liquor boxes, others labeled theatrical supplies.

The one at eye level to my right read: *White Feathers: 1 Gross.* Ghostly tendrils still clung to the tape along one edge.

I pushed my way forward through the cardboard corridor, so narrow that my shoulders brushed it on either side. It went straight for a few steps then branched, one side toward the window and (I presumed) the bed area, the other snaking toward her sitting room.

I opted for the latter.

At the threshold between the two rooms, near a rack of cocktail dresses, I sought another light switch, but it was just as fruitless. The air smelled of dust and perfume and the ancient fabric that I kept brushing against, as though it were reaching out for me as I passed.

The next room was even darker, the windows completely blocked by long curtains. I was using my cell phone as a flashlight by now, holding it out between my fingertips. It startled me when it rang.

I glanced at the screen. My mother.

I answered, standing there in the dusty darkness that smelled like Grandmother. "Yes?"

"I need you to pick me up at the airport at 1:15," my mother said.

"Today?"

"Of course today! I'm about to get on the plane. I'm flying on United, flight 323. Do you need me to repeat all that so you can write it down?"

"Why are you coming?"

"So I can help you."

Suspicion seized me. "Where are you staying?"

A pause, as though my question was in some foreign language that required translation before it could be processed. "With you. Aren't you staying there at the house?"

I imagined my mother "helping" me. It made my throat tight. All my life I'd watched the two of them do battle. Now my mother had come to crow over a victory that consisted of simply having outlived the other. Or, worse, like the others—the agents, Eterno—she wanted something here but would not tell me what.

I steeled myself and said, "No, you can't do that. I'll find you a hotel."

"Don't be ridiculous. Why on earth can't I stay there?"

My mind cast about for excuses. There must be some reason.

"It's a legal thing," I said. "The will dictated that I had to sort the place by myself. No help."

Which was only semi-true, but my mother had never been particularly detail-oriented, so I hoped she'd buy this.

She did, although she liked it not at all. "You can pick me up in the morning and I can help, at least," she said. "I know where a lot of her things came from originally and can help you sort out what's valuable and what's not."

I'd bought myself a reprieve, so I didn't fuss. My mother loved Vegas and could easily be distracted by promises of going to see a music (never magic) show, or dinner at a club. She loved to gamble—for a long time I'd thought the falling out between them was over one of my mother's gambling debts, but neither had indicated that this was true. It was the sort of thing, I knew, that my grandmother would have loved to reproach my mother with.

I put the phone away and stood in the darkness, listening. But the only sounds were the long slow creaks of the house, the scrape of the wind against the roof, the distant roar of the air conditioning unit trying to keep the downstairs cool.

I stepped forward into the darkened room. Something glimmered on the other side.

⌒

Perhaps I should have known that she'd leave me whatever it was that she thought most important there in the parlor, where she'd spent so many hours practicing sleight of hand or playing the tall harp that sat beside her fainting couch. It was evident that she'd passed a great deal of her recent time here. A jumble of metal puzzles punctuated the coffee table's surface, along with several years' worth of entertainment trade magazines. Even retired, she'd believed in keeping up with competition in the field.

She'd placed it on the little rosewood and ebony table that used to hold a foot-tall statue of the goddess Athena. A quart-sized mason jar, but its glass glowed with an oily, green-tinged white light. Not as though something inside the jar was glowing, but as though the glass itself was glowing, shining into and trebling itself to almost a lamp-like brilliance. The shadows it cast wobbled over the room's interior, unexpectedly free of carton stacks.

I went to the table's edge and faced the jar. It was sealed. A label on the side was written in my grandmother's careful penmanship.

"Susan Day's ghost, 2/22/63," it said. Propped against the jar's base, an index card with words in the same handwriting: "She'll help you."

I touched the side of the jar. Despite its almost radioactive shine, it was cold as the moon—so cold I was worried that my skin might freeze to it.

Frost crystals furred the iron lid's edges as well.

"But what do I *do* with you?" I wondered, staring at it. I half-expected the jar to answer, but it remained mute.

If I unscrewed the lid—which seemed like the logical thing to do, particularly given the lack of instructions—would it free the ghost?

Was this the object that everyone was looking for? How did they know she had such a thing? And what had she used it for, if she had used it at all? I thought back on the cellophane-wrapped bars I'd found stacked in one bathroom:

enough tangerine-scented soaps to cleanse the entire city, so old the soap had gone blotchy and brown.

Had the ghost been waiting all this time to be freed? What if it were angry? I pulled my hand back.

Research was called for.

Grandmother's library was literally impassable, so high and closely stacked were the cartons of books. Many were books from fans, with personal notes to her written inside the cover; others were histories of stage magic with footnotes, sometimes entire chapters, covering her life. There'd been three Gloria Aim biographies published. Only one was authorized, but you wouldn't know that from the number of boxes of the other two she'd stashed away here.

I brought the jar with me. To protect myself from its chill, I'd wrapped it in a small throw blanket I'd picked up from the fainting couch. Even wrapped away, its light glowed, lighting the cloth from the inside. I put it on the table near the door and began to move cartons, clearing a path to the eastern wall.

Most stage magicians pursue the trappings of the real deal, true magic, as though it's a mandate, some geas that comes with the job. Grandmother had been no exception, and the shelves on the eastern wall held manuscripts that had belonged to John Dee and Roger Bacon, witches' grimoires, and parchments, old long before Las Vegas ever bloomed in the desert.

There was no card catalog or indexing system of course. I ran my finger along the spines, letting them bump past, until I found *On Ghosts*, a slim book with a blue-paper wrapper covered with spirals. It was written by some San Franciscan I remembered coming to the house once or twice when I was a child, although I didn't remember them talking about ghosts. That seemed as good as a starting point as any. I pulled down a few more titles, stacked them on a table, and sat down to think. My mother would be in a few hours, and I needed to prepare my ground as carefully as any military campaigner.

Some of this sounds hyperbolic, or as though my mother was some Crawfordesque vision of rage. In truth, she was a rather passive creature, but at the same time, one who saw the world through a constant lens of negativity. Everything was bad to my mother; there was always a worm at the heart of the rose, and I'd been no exception.

She was happy enough to leave me to my own devices as a child. Most of my meals were TV dinners, indeed eaten in front of the TV, while she was out working.

She was skewed, my mother, in a way I was incapable of seeing until I left the house and saw some other families in action. Other people didn't call their parents by their first name. Other people celebrated things like birthdays and Christmas; my mother found them cliché. Other people had parents who came to school plays and games and parent-teacher nights.

Just thinking about her tore me up. Being around her was a battle.

I'd keep anything that I didn't want her to see in my room. I had the great circle of keys, after all, and that was the only key to the room. I'd stashed the metal leg in the room, and now I took the mason jar there too, but moved by some impulse, I hid that even deeper, putting it in the very back of the towel cupboard and closing the door, extinguishing the jar's light.

I clicked the key in the lock.

Hiding things from my mother as though she were an opponent or enemy; even dead, my grandmother continued their war.

My phone rang while I was waiting in the airport parking

lot for my mother, whose plane had been delayed a half hour. A start-up I'd never heard of, offering me a job.

Flattered, I said I was available, but not until the house was sorted, at least a month off.

I didn't think the request remarkable in any way, but they got huffy, pushed me. An amazing salary—but only if I could start the following week.

I tried to find out the rationale behind the hurry, but the recruiter told me nothing, just pressed harder. Finally, I forced a regretful no—the sum was very large indeed—and hung up, glad that it hadn't happened in my mother's presence.

But it was odd, that pressure. Surely it would be paranoid of me to think agent Forest capable of creating a scheme to manipulate me that way.

Wouldn't it?

My mother arrived in a flutter of scarves and an ensemble utterly unsuitable for the heat.

"I'd forgotten how awful it is here," she said, directing the attendant to put her four bags in the back of my car. "For the love of God, get me somewhere air-conditioned."

I asked how the flight had been, and she told me, in too much detail.

"I've booked you in the Luxor," I said. "Figured you might as well enjoy the Vegas lifestyle while you're here." It also put a thirty-minute drive buffer between us. Without a car, she'd end up relying on me for rides and that was enough distance that trips wouldn't be trivial back-and-forths.

I could see her calculating all that, but also putting it up against the lure of having gambling facilities just an elevator away. She gave me an *I know what you're doing* look, but just murmured, "Okay."

"After I drop you there, I'll come back in a couple of hours," I added, "and get you for dinner. What would you like?"

"That good Chinese place Eterno sometimes takes us to," she said. "Have you seen him?"

"I just ran into him at the grocery store yesterday. We had coffee."

"Is he well?"

"Same as always. Larger than life. He asked if I'd ever wondered if he was my grandfather."

She snorted. "Of course he's not."

The assuredness of her words surprised me. "Then you do know who my grandfather—your father—was? I thought Grandmother never told you."

"I've met my father." She was smiling faintly as she looked out the front window.

"Is he still alive?"

Silence.

"Why don't I get to know?" I said. "You do, for chrissake."

"It's complicated." She was still smiling. She loved being the one to hold all the cards. My grandmother's death had shifted our dynamic.

Once again, I wondered if I might replace Grandmother as the opponent mother centered her life around. Better to avoid that.

I reached over to touch her hand. "I'm sorry. You don't need to tell me. I wanted to say how much I appreciated your coming." Placate her now, ask her again later, and see if I could catch her at the right unguarded moment.

She said, "What have you found so far?"

"A lot of junk. Things don't seem to have appreciated in value the way you'd think. And the climate of the house turns out to be bad for paper. Everything's falling apart."

"Susan Day had some valuable old things," my mother said. We had entered the Strip now. Even washed out in the daylight, it looked vibrant, charged with electricity and money. My mother's distant gaze drifted over the hordes of sweating tourists.

"Some very valuable old things," she repeated. "Antiques. Military memorabilia from her time as a spy."

I thought of the swastika emblazoned hand. "What sort of military memorabilia?"

Her head snapped around. "Why? What have you found?"

Her reaction made me wary. I backpedaled. "Nothing other than newspapers," I lied. "Perhaps I've been looking in the wrong places. I'm still only a few rooms in."

She relaxed. "Well, now that I'm here to help it'll go faster," she said. "After dinner, maybe we'll take a look."

I called Eterno to see if he wanted to go with us, but he'd already made plans.

"You're capable of dealing with your mother on your own, kiddo," he told me.

I winced. Was I really that obvious?

"I want to talk to you," I said.

"What about?"

"Ghosts."

"Huh?" he said. The lack of hesitation made me think it wasn't Susan Day's ghost he was after, after all.

No, it must be the mechanical limbs that everyone was looking for.

Over dinner, I pushed alcohol on my mother, telling her she should have a few glasses of wine in order to unwind and adjust to the time change.

"Well," she said, "all right" and let herself be talked into an after-dinner liqueur as well. I figured she'd be sleepy and a little buzzed on the way back, that she wouldn't object when I dropped her at the hotel.

But only a few blocks from the restaurant, she said, "We aren't going to the house?"

"It's late," I said. "You must be tired."

"Is it going to be like this the whole visit?"

I stonewalled. "What do you mean?"

"She's dead, Persephone. You don't need to protect her from me anymore."

I sighed. "What do you want, mother?"

"For you to be happy. When have I wanted anything else?"

"Plenty of times."

She fell into offended silence. She wanted me to overflow with apology, to kowtow to her, but I was digging in my heels this time. I was too old for anyone but myself to rule my life.

Even though I was here sorting through houses at a dead woman's whim. But I thrust that thought away.

We drove back to the hotel in icy silence.

"I've got errands in the morning," I said. "I'll come by at lunchtime.

"We'll see," she said, snipping off the words, but she relented and leaned over to hug me, a long fierce pressure that meant all the affection she could never say out loud.

When I got back to the house, I realized I'd lost my keys somewhere in the course of the evening. It was my little key ring, the one to the outside doors. I kept the vast key ring that controlled all the inner doors to the house up in my room. I called a locksmith, but he couldn't come for a few hours. So I made the most of it and called Eterno, who didn't mind letting me come over with two coffees and a sack of doughnuts.

⤳

I said, "She left me a ghost."

His eyebrows rose, startled. "A ghost."

"Susan Day's ghost, to be precise."

He rubbed the side of a finger against his chin. His kitchen was small but immaculate. It looked rarely eaten in, and when I'd tried to find milk for my coffee, the fridge only yielded old takeout cartons and a glass pitcher of water.

"She was there at the deathbed, I know," he mused. "But I always thought she was there to protect Day's ghost from being taken, not to take it herself. Damn, that's cold."

"What would she have taken it for?" I asked.

"Hmm. Let me think of how to put it." He pinched his forehead. "Some people take them to talk to. But most, well, they're a source of power. Think about if you were building a house. You'd need things to power systems, like a furnace for a heating system or a breaker box for the electricity? A ghost can act like one of those. It's why most magicians try to get them. You put them inside other things."

I gazed at him.

He looked back. "What?"

I gestured helplessly. "I expected there to be more denial, more telling me I was being paranoid or crazy."

He shook his head then leaned forward to touch my hand in reassurance. "Most magicians know better than deny the Hidden World's existence, once someone's stumbled across it. Or have been brought to it, in your case."

"As long as we're being all open and aboveboard," I said, "what's this piece of war memorabilia everyone's looking for?"

His attention sharpened. "Who else is looking for it?"

"Who isn't?" I said. "That's why my mother's out here, I'm sure."

He started to relax until I said, "And some government agents as well."

His shoulders slumped in a sigh. "Very well. Susan Day had an automaton she'd pilfered from the Nazis."

"Pilfered parts or in its entirety?" I asked, thinking of what I'd found so far.

"Oh, its entirety. I've talked to it, back in the day."

"What? When?"

"Your grandmother had it up and running up until you were born. Something went wrong with it. I don't know whether the problem was mechanical—I always presumed it was, though—or something else."

I blinked. "Why would Grandmother have disassembled it?"

He squinted at me. "Your mother never said anything about it? She was obsessed with that thing."

"What do you mean, obsessed with it?"

"She'd sit and talk to it like it was a person. Said its name was Heinrich. She spent hours with it."

"It couldn't talk back?"

"Sure, it could. In German. Pretty limited vocabulary, too. Your mom was a weird kid. Must be where you got it from." He beamed at me.

I said, "Why did Grandmother hate card tricks?"

Eterno shuffled the cards in his hand. "It was a philosophical issue. Why do gamblers play cards?"

"Because they can gamble on them. They're random."

He shook his head and the cards in his hands flurried in reproach. "The gamblers bet on the future. Thinking they can predict it with the right system or luck charm. Because what are cards but patterns?"

He leaned forward, lip tugging in a half smile. He was enjoying the chance to play pedantic grandfather.

"I don't understand what you mean," I said impatiently. I don't like mumbo jumbo, frills for the sake of frills, and this all seemed a part of that.

"You'll understand with time," he said. "Patterns are

everything. What is the automaton but a pattern of choices programmed in, shaped by its origin? You need to keep that in mind, Persephone. It was a war machine, and it remains one, no matter how many flowers you make it hold. Your grandmother understood that, eventually."

"So you do know why she took it apart," I guessed.

He sighed. "Yes, but I didn't want to upset you. Your grandmother overheard your mother talking with it. They were discussing whether or not it could override or replace someone's personality, provide it with a human body. Swap the two. Your mother wanted it to, but Heinrich was reluctant to give up its metal form and the power that brought. Nonetheless, your grandmother thought it best to remove him as an influence. Your mother was . . . well, to say upset would be to understate it by quite a bit. She was furious. And when she figured out where your grandmother had left its head, she took it—left the house with you and the head and never looked back."

He looked at me earnestly. "We both know she's a little crazy. But this is the center of that craziness. She won't stop at anything to restore him. I suspect that now that your grandmother's gone, she thinks it's possible again, and she's determined to do it."

⤳

This time when I got back to the house, the front door to the Tudor was a few inches ajar. Someone had come across my keys and somehow known to bring them here. Then I remembered my mother's unexpectedly tight hug. How stupid could I have been? She knew how to call a taxi.

"Mother?" I called as I entered. I thought she'd be up in Grandmother's bedroom but didn't see her there. My bedroom door was open, the closet and dresser plundered. I didn't have time to check the bathroom—I heard a crash from down in the library and went to investigate.

She'd pulled over a bookcase in her search. A pillowcase, whose lumpy exterior attested that it held the limbs already gathered, lay at her feet. As I came in, she said, "A hand and a leg, that's all you've found so far?"

"You outright admit that you went through my bedroom?"

"It's mine by rights. She'd promised it to me."

"Possession is nine-tenths of the law."

She pointed at the pillowcase. "Well, now I possess those."

"I want you out of here," I said.

Her face softened. Her hair was spiked and mussed. She'd been rushing, hunting as hard as she could in the time before I got back.

"Honey," she said. "Don't let her get to you even after her death. She was so good at playing us off each other."

"We're all good at that," I said. "It's a family trait. Stop fucking around, mother. Are you stealing these things from me or not?"

Her eyes widened with indignation. "Stealing! As I said, she promised them to me—"

"But didn't include them in the will," I pointed out.

She dropped her gaze to the faded carpet. "She got confused when she got older."

"You two went to war, and she wrote you out entirely," I said. "I'm sure that those circumstances negated any previous arrangement, in her mind."

"And now you've got a chance to set that right," she snapped.

I moved out of her way. "Very well. Take them and go. But leave my keys here."

I didn't put it past her not to have duplicated them, but

she'd only had the outside ones before getting here. I'd go ahead and have the locksmith swap out those locks.

Once she was gone, I checked the bathroom cupboard. Susan Day's mason jar was there. I'd kept that much safe, at least.

What had my grandmother wanted from me, in asking me to sort out this house, this jumbled mass of objects? Why give me no instructions, not even a starting point?

But she had, though, hadn't she? I thought of the card that had been with the jar. *She'll help you.*

Grandmother had expected me to know how to access that knowledge.

You put them inside other things, Eterno had said.

I thought of the banks of dolls, the blank gazes.

Now I understood what to do.

～

After the locksmith had come and gone, I secured the outside doors and got started. I checked my phone. Nothing from my mother yet, but that was to be expected. She'd never be the first to yield in a battle with me. All her life, she'd had little control over things around her, and I'd been the first thing she'd had total, utter power over. I'd been the battleground for them all my life.

Now my mother waited, knowing that sooner or later I'd come to plead with her, that I couldn't cut her off entirely, not with my grandmother, the entire other half of my support system, gone.

Ever since college I'd lived a nomadic existence, consulting, six months here, three months there, enjoying a life of hotel rooms, clean and free of family history. Every other place seemed to become so fraught, so full of furniture funded by presents, obligations shipped to me. I'd had to defend that existence from mother and Grandmother, over and over again, in order to stay as free of them as I could, but the two were always there in the back of my head, always as close as my own hand.

In a college class, I ran across a quote: *110% of American families are dysfunctional.* Certainly mine was.

When I searched through the dolls, I was able to find one that even resembled the pictures of Susan Day, down to the blonde hairstyle.

A large doll, complete with a talking mechanism. Would that matter? I didn't think it could hurt, at least.

I set the doll beside the jar. I looked between the two of them. My grandmother had left no instructions. Did that mean that none were necessary? Sometimes you had to just forge ahead and see what happened.

I used an old sweater of Grandmother's to cushion my fingers from the coldness of the lid. It was difficult to budge at first. I thought about home remedies like running it under the hot water tap or turning it upside down and rapping the lid on the floor. But that all seemed so practical; so unmystical.

But finally, it yielded under my grip. I clenched it under an elbow, ignoring the cold's bite, and turned it around and around until it fell away from my fingers and clattered on the floor.

Despite the outside glow, when I looked inside the glass, it was as dark as midnight, as though the jar held an infinite amount of space, stretching away forever. As I stared into the depths, a blue light rushed toward me, as though from very far away, coming closer, closer.

I pulled my head away from the jar just in time. The blue light shot out of the jar and splashed silently, brilliantly against the high ceiling, splintering into a thousand shards of light and illuminating the room as brightly as though I stood in sunlight and not in the house's interior.

Then, just as suddenly, all those shards converged on the doll in front of me. The speed and force of the light made it seem as though the doll should shudder at the impact, but it didn't move at all as the light dove inside it, vanishing as it did so, although some still seeped out from the doll's body, shining out from its eyes and mouth, and from the seams between its jointed limbs.

Now it twitched, now it moved. The eyes flew open and fixed on me, burning a deep turquoise color. "Who are you?" the doll said. Its voice was high and squeaky and not at all human.

"My name is Persephone. Gloria Aim was my grandmother."

"Was? Then Gloria is dead? What year is it?"

I told her and the doll let out a hiss that must've been a sigh and sagged back where it sat. "So long." It fixed its eyes on me again. "What is it that you want?"

"My grandmother left me your jar and said that you would help me."

"It is typical of your grandmother that she would've shut me in a jar for over half a century, and then expected me to help out whoever happened to open it," the doll said. It was amazing how dryly cynical such a squeaky little voice could be.

"It's about an object that used to belong to you," I said. "An automaton, a German one."

"Ah, Heinrich." Now the doll's voice seemed gentler. "Where is he now?"

"He's in pieces, actually. Pieces scattered all over this house and two others. I was hoping you'd be able to help me locate him."

"I might be able to. But how did he come to be dismantled?"

"Your protégé did it. Why, I don't know. I haven't been able to piece that together yet."

"It's no surprise. It could've been for any number of reasons. He was made to function as a killing machine—not a personal servant."

"Why didn't you turn him over to the government after you stole him?"

"He begged me not to. He knew that they'd take him apart in order to figure out how he'd been made, in order to make more things like him. And having seen what he could do, I wasn't sure that either side should have him."

"So you just stuck him away in a closet."

She shrugged. "I didn't dismantle him," she pointed out.

I hesitated. "Can you talk to my grandmother?" I asked. "There, on the Other Side."

"It doesn't work like that," she said. "There's not some sort of telepathic phone line that all the dead get automatically hooked into."

"Oh." I'd hoped to find out what my grandmother had intended from her own lips. I wondered what had happened to her ghost. She'd died very suddenly, a heart attack that had overtaken her on an evening out. No one had sat in her hospital room to defend or take her ghost. It would have just gone on and done whatever it was that ordinary ghosts did, when there was no one to interrupt their death with mason jars.

"What was it like in the jar?"

"What?" the doll said blankly.

I pointed at the open jar on the table. "What was it like? Could you see anything, hear anything?"

"Oh. No. Nothing at all." She sounded unperturbed at the thought, but I shivered, imagining decades of being shut in a jar with no one but myself for company.

"Will you show me where the pieces are now? Of Heinrich?"

She nodded. The glass eyes closed and a bit of light darted out from her mouth. It hung in the air in front of me. I stepped toward it, and it dipped away, leading me on my quest.

It took less time than I'd thought but the pieces were strewn between all three houses. The weirdest were the genitals, which she'd hidden inside a grandfather clock. Burnished aluminum and brass, looking like a casting from a Greek statue. Like the hand, the weight seemed to wobble oddly when I picked them up.

When I had all of the pieces, the shard of light led me back to the doll. I expected it to speak again but instead the light dashed inside the mason jar and hung there. Unsure what else to do, I sealed it again. While the lid was off, the glass was at room temperature; the minute it grated closed, the temperature began to drop.

I sorted through what I'd found. I'd thought I had all the pieces, except for what my mother had taken and the head, but I was missing a hand, the right one. I was sure I hadn't missed one in the houses. Did my mother have that as well? I chewed my lip, trying to figure it out.

I could only guess at my mother's motivations in wanting the brass automaton so fiercely that she was prepared to give me up for it. Did she, like Eterno, think it somehow her father? Was it *possible* that it was partially her father? How could that physically be?

It was a whole new side to my mother, one I'd never seen before, but now that I knew she'd had the head with her all along, it began to explain so much. She'd always preferred to be alone in her bedroom, was fiercely defensive of her privacy. And sometimes she'd agree to something and then go away for a while and come back to renege on that agreement, saying that she'd rethought it.

The sensation was like discovering that someone you knew was a secret addict—suddenly so much fell into place, suddenly made sense in a way it never had before.

All through my childhood, I'd had a second parent directing things, I just hadn't realized it. I'd pitied my mother for what I'd thought her loneliness, and now I found she'd had a truer companion than most, someone who literally couldn't leave her.

I made a call to Eterno, and then called my mother. She'd known I would. She took her time answering the phone, deliberately, I'm sure.

I said, "I want to meet up. I have the rest of the parts. But I want something for them. I want you to sign a paper saying you don't want any other part of the estate."

Brief silence on the other end of the line. She was calculating what my words meant in her head. Wondering if there was there something else that she should want, that she just wasn't aware of? But in the end, she made the choice that I thought she would.

"Where should we meet?" she asked.

I gave her the name of the rendezvous, a good thirty minutes from her hotel. "We can meet at four. I'm not going to pick you up. You'll have to take a taxi."

"All right," she said, and hung up without uttering another word.

I called Eterno again. "All right," I said. "She'll be there. After I don't show up, she'll start to get suspicious. Show up then. You can distract her for a little while. Call me when she leaves."

And then I set off to burglarize my mother's hotel room.

⌒

In the end, all the careful preparation I'd been going over in my head in the car, careful, obsessive, planning for every contingency, was unnecessary. I'd made my mother's reservation and picked up her card, so the desk clerk knew me. I said, "My key card's stopped working—I had it in my cell phone case, would that mess with it?"

"I always say, the smarter the phone, the dumber the card," said the clerk.

It was all going so well that I couldn't help but suspect that things would go pear-shaped at any moment.

But as I got farther into the hotel, I found myself untensing. I hadn't realized what it was like in grandmother's house, how the weight of things pressed down on me. Here, in this cream and lemon-colored hallway that smelled of disinfectant, where dust dare not gather and silverfish dare not twitch, I found myself floating down the hallway to where her *Do Not Disturb* sign hung on the doorknob.

When I opened the door, I returned to earth. Mom had always been a nester, although she'd never gotten as bad as Grandmother, and the interior of this hotel room showed it. Heaps of clothing covered the floor, along with delivery food containers and Starbucks cups. A fly oscillated between the gauzy curtain and the window glass like a miniature chain saw.

How had she managed to accumulate so much in the short time she'd been here?

On the dresser there was an odd metal plate that seemed to be the same technology as the things that I'd found so far. It was octagonal, solid, a good four inches thick and eight inches around, so heavy that it was hard to lift. In the center was a round divot, about five inches across.

Under the bed, I found an old suitcase, the sort that holds a wig or a hat. I pulled it out—it was promisingly heavy. The labels on it were in mother's handwriting, fine and spidery, edged with unnecessary curlicues. I remembered this suitcase. She always had it.

I had to smash the lock to get the case open. Inside, there it was.

I took the head out of the case.

It was heavy. Heavier than a normal head? I had no real way of judging, but it felt like a jar full of quarters, contents shifting as I tilted it. I held it neck upward, and a bead of silvery liquid—an oily, mercury-like substance—welled in an indention in the metal plate that was the neck's base, creating a small bowl studded with pockmarks, intricate circuitry etching the interior of each circle.

The eyelids clicked open and it *looked* at me.

I was so startled I dropped it. It fell to the dusty shag with a clunk then landed on its side, a few feet away, staring at the wall. It didn't speak, but its gaze shifted from side to side, assessing its surroundings.

I went over to it from behind and picked it up, still facing away from me. I put it down on the plate on the dresser, which now made sense to me.

"Persephone," the head said.

A chill ran down my spine. I knew that voice from somewhere, somewhere distant, only half-remembered.

"What do you want?" I asked.

"Why are you here?" It spoke in English, but it did have a faint German accent.

"To take back the pieces of you that Mother stole." I stared at him. "Looks like I found a bonus too."

He was silent for a moment as though calculating. "You will reunite me with my body?"

"Does that make it okay, if I'm going to?" I was curious—clearly this thing had little sense of loyalty.

"Perhaps," it said.

My phone rang.

I answered with a sense of ease. Even if Mom sped back, I'd have plenty of time. But Eterno's voice was urgent. "She left some time ago, but my phone died. You've got maybe five minutes."

Adrenaline jolted me. "Well," I told the head as I gathered it and the limbs up. "If you keep quiet, perhaps I'll reunite you with your body. Shout or cry out, and I'll do nothing of the sort."

"I will cooperate," the head said, and it kept its word as I left the hotel through a back stairway, the limbs and head in a bundle beneath my left arm. I heard my mother entering even as I was exiting, and so I kept moving until I was well away.

Once we were in the car, the head kept trying to talk to me as we drove along. I turned the air conditioner up but still felt flushed. Feverish and panicked.

"Why do I recognize your voice?" I asked it.

"This isn't the first time we've spoken," it said. "When you were a child, we talked more than once."

"While you were still with my grandmother or after my mother had stolen you from her?"

It was silent, as though it lacked the words. Finally, it said, "Both. But your mother forbade me to make myself known to you once you were old enough to talk."

"Why?" What had my mother feared would happen if the head and I conversed?

It pursed its lips and rolled its eyes in the equivalent of a shrug. "I don't remember," it said, voice bland as unbuttered toast.

"Bullshit," I said, and we didn't speak again, all the way

home. Even there, I refrained from putting it in the same house as the limbs. I didn't know if it could control them, but I thought there must have been a reason why my grandmother had scattered them so thoroughly.

I went back up to the parlor. Again, I opened the mason jar. Again the lights dove and splashed.

"You know you can only do this three times, right?" the doll asked me.

"Nope. That would have been a good thing to mention that first time though."

The doll's silence was as eloquent as a shrug.

"What happens the third time?" I asked.

"I will answer questions for a third time."

There was a pause. I had that maddening *I'm-missing-something* feeling that usually only occurred during encounters with my mother or grandmother.

"What about the fourth time?" I said cautiously.

"After the third time, I will vanish into the afterlife."

"Got it. Three times only. So let's get answering. What about Heinrich? Can he reassemble himself?"

"If the pieces are close enough together, yes."

"How would she have disassembled him?"

"There is a failsafe mechanism."

"What does it look like? Can you find it the way you did him?"

"I cannot. It looks like nine small beans made of purple metal. They snap together. Squeeze once to disassemble him." She hesitated. "Squeeze twice to wipe his personality and memories."

"Why didn't you do that?"

"I told you. He begged me. He said he'd been condemned to a life of torment and asked me to give him a respite."

My mind raced over what I'd seen. I thought of the odd

purple succulents. "I might know where those are." I hesitated but I couldn't think of anything else to ask Susan Day.

"I'm sorry my grandmother killed you and put your ghost in a jar," I blurted.

"Are you sure you're Gloria's granddaughter?"

"I think I am, but," I admitted, "by now nothing would surprise me."

My grandmother's face appeared in reproachful memory, and I thought of all she'd done for me over the years. "No. That's not fair. I know she was my grandmother. I loved her. And you must have liked—maybe even loved—her once, mustn't you have? After all, she was your protégé."

"She was." The doll's glassy eyes were fixed on some point in the middle distance. "I did. But your grandmother's façade was much more loveable than what lay underneath. Underneath she was cold steel, couldn't be trusted to work to anyone's advantage but her own. Perhaps as her own flesh and blood you occupied a special place in her heart, but I could claim no similar advantage. I thought I could—she let me think so—for a long time. It wasn't until she pressed the pillow over my face that I realized I'd been deluding myself all that time."

I could believe every word of it. Grandmother had been ruthless beyond anyone else I knew, with the exception of my mother.

But was it really true? I thought of the crates of Day's belongings arriving, with the word that she'd willed them to my grandmother. Object after object, the beginning of the hoarding; the beginning of her guilt eroding the glitter.

"I'll make this right," I said.

"How will you recompense me for the years she snatched away?" the doll demanded.

"I don't know," I said, "But I will."

∽

My mother had left a voicemail screaming vituperation at me on my phone.

I listened to it, shaken, and did not erase it. I'd save it for any time I was tempted to give in to her again.

I was right about the purple planters. Not about how easy it would be to get to them. The courtyard plants grew together in tangled clumps and plants had unexpected thorns, wickedly long, that stung like wasps. One by one, I wrestled the pots free from their entanglement. Each was too overgrown to come out of the pot easily, and so I smashed them, picking through the clumps of dirty roots to find, each time, the metal bean that Susan Day had described, tangled in the long tendrils. I couldn't bear to leave the plants there, outside their pots on the concrete, so I replanted them in the narrow strip of soil near the central fountain.

My mother followed the phone call with an appearance within the hour.

"I'll call the police and tell them you stole from me," she threatened from the other side of the door.

"Oh please," I said. "You can't prove that anything here is yours."

"Not true. I have a certificate of ownership for a valuable antique automaton, a valuation signed by Christie's in London. It describes it all in detail."

"Well, good luck finding it in here, that's all I can say."

"I'll keep this place so tied up that you will never be able to dispose of a single thing. You'll be saddled with inheritance taxes for the value of the dolls, with no way to pay it."

This was more convincing than any of her other threats. I wouldn't be able to sell anything, according to the terms of the will, until I'd finished doing a complete evaluation of the houses and the estate holdings. I wondered again what my grandmother had been thinking. Surely there had been more rationale behind it than to complicate my life as much as possible? You might have thought a true magician would have had some clue that her death would coincide with the tail end of a time on my own calendar when I was decidedly short on funds.

"Do whatever you need to do," I told her, "but in fifteen minutes I'm calling the cops and having you tossed out of here."

It was a good thing I went upstairs after that. While Susan Day had been right that the pieces kept in different houses couldn't reassemble into each other, she'd forgotten to tell me that pieces in the same house could—and would—combine. An arm was pulling the chest across the floor, the hand exploring everything. It had pulled the coverlet off the bed and torn it into strips that littered the floor.

Apart from each other, the limbs had been lifeless. Just odd toys. But combined, they'd taken on a menacing aspect that made me use the metal beads to force them apart, then lock one in a trunk, the other in a closet on the other side of the house.

My mother shouted for a while outside, then went away.

Meanwhile I did some experimenting with the metal beads. They'd snapped together into a strange, hollow little ball, which could be compressed in the hand but with difficulty. Doing so did make the pieces fly apart from each other, with enough force that several inches separated them.

I went through and rearranged the configuration of pieces as best I could, and when I had finished, I realized why my grandmother had hidden them the way she did, in order to keep the limbs as far apart from each other as possible.

With the addition of the head, it was almost impossible to

rearrange. I called Agent Forest. I said, "I don't know where that memorabilia is yet that you're looking for, but I do have a suspicion. My mother showed me a certificate of authenticity for something described as a "valuable antique automaton." Might that be the sort of thing you're looking for?"

"Indeed," he breathed out. "You've done us a valuable service, Ms. Aim."

It wouldn't buy me much time, but a little.

Was there any way to just turn the thing off? I went to where I'd hidden the head in the basement, wrapped in blankets in a trunk so it wouldn't be able to call out to anyone. I took the beads with me, held them in one hand as I unwrapped it with the other.

"Why shouldn't I just erase you?" I asked it.

"Why shouldn't you just give me back to your mother?"

"You're a war machine. You have no ethics. You're made to destroy."

"I was made for many reasons. My creator, Doktor Eisenmacher, made me in his dead son's image, and taught me how to do all the things young Otto Eisenmacher had been adept in, such as conversation and being able to play the pianoforte. But yes, I am also made to create and execute military strategies."

"How did Susan Day come to steal you?"

It laughed. "Steal? Eisenmacher *gave* me to her. He said he didn't want to see me used for war and that she'd keep me safe. He didn't know she was a spy, but it made no difference. She told her superiors I'd been destroyed and kept me for herself."

I fingered the construction of beads uneasily. Part of me felt that this thing had controlled my mother all my life, and that if it were gone, maybe we'd have a chance to heal our relationship.

"I'm valuable," the head said. "I have the knowledge of a thousand libraries accumulated in my brain."

"Did he include psychological theories in the programming?" I said bitterly. "Is that how you learned to manipulate my mother so well?"

I meant it as a joke, but it took me seriously. "All the mental theories. And the data our scientists gathered."

"Data?" I said softly.

"They had thousands of subjects. They learned so much."

I couldn't help it. My fingers spasmed on the device once. But the second time it was by choice.

Something clicked and whirred inside the head and it fell silent. I didn't bother putting it back in the trunk but, instead, took it back to my bedroom.

A knock at the door. When I opened it, Eterno stood there. I blinked at him. He said, "For Heaven's sake, child, invite me in."

"Is it like vampires, where you can't come in unless I invite you?" I said with interest, but he shook his head.

"It's because I believe in courtesy," he said wryly. He looked around with fondness as he entered.

"What were you and Grandmother to each other?" I demanded.

"The truth—I am your grandfather, but only partly," he admitted. "That—machine helped influence your mother in the womb as well. At least, she absorbed some of his energies. She knew it, too, somehow. Even as a baby, if he was there in the room, anywhere, even when she couldn't see or hear him, her head would be turned his way."

"Why did she keep him?"

"Your grandmother? I don't think you understand what the thing is like when it's whole. It's charming. Handsome. Powerful."

"You said its vocabulary was limited last time."

"At first it was, but the thing was self-adjusting. Self-teaching."

"You don't need to worry about it anymore," I said.

Another knock at the door, just as the teakettle went off.

"You get it," I said. "It's the agents, I suspect."

Eterno frowned but did not demur. I went to make tea.

When I came back, it was not the agents there with Eterno, but my mother. She stood there, oddly enough, with the missing metal hand pointed into his side. Apparently Eterno knew more than I did about its capabilities; he was keeping very still.

She said to me, "Where is he? Where's Heinrich?"

"Not here," I said.

She jabbed the finger into Eterno's ribs. "Bring him here or I kill the old man."

"He's your father."

"No. Heinrich's my father. Bring him to me."

What could I do?

"He's upstairs," I said. "I can go get him."

Her eyes glittered at me. How had I never guessed the depths of her lunacy?

"All right," she said, "but if you try some trickery, you should know I *will* kill him." She pulled back her hand and pointed downward. With a *crack!* and smell of electricity, a projectile whizzed from the barrel, shooting Eterno in the leg. He cried out and went to his knees, then dropped forward onto his hands. She stood there with the hand aimed anew at the back of his head and nodded in challenge at me.

"All right," I said hastily. "All right." I went upstairs.

What to do? But a plan glimmered in my head.

I might have removed Heinrich's personality, but I still had his body.

What can you do with a ghost? *You can put them in things,* Eterno said in my head. And I hadn't restored Day to her jar yet.

⸏

When my mother saw the automaton descending the stairway, she rushed forward, pushing me out of the way. I went to Eterno, who lay in a spreading pool of blood.

"Stay with me, old man," I said to him.

He gripped my hand. His lips were gray beneath the snowy beard. "I'll try," he rasped.

I looked at the blue dazzle in the automaton's eyes.

"Now," I said.

I expected the ghost to disarm her. Or something, anything. Not reach out, disregarding the flash bang of the shots, to take her by the neck and snap it. Not to drop her to the floor.

Susan Day turned to me. She might have said some word of explanation. Or recrimination. Some lengthy thing about justice served. But she spared me that.

Eterno squeezed my hand. I pulled my stare from the automaton and fumbled for my cell phone.

⸏

The police had plenty of questions, but in the end no proof, only suspicions. I took the United States up on its offer to inventory and appraise Grandmother's belongings, which saved me some amount of money, a whole lot of time, and an incalculable amount of sweat and stink. While they worked, I had my mother cremated and arranged a small, tasteful memorial service.

I asked people instead of sending flowers to make a donation to the same museum of stage magic that took so many of Grandmother's things as donations.

A company suggested by Agent Forrest packed up other stuff and sent it off for online auctions. He and his fellow agent were disappointed that they'd found no trace of the war relics they were seeking but, between the two of us, Eterno and I had been able to cook up enough false leads to keep them busy for a while.

Eterno showed up to oversee my final move out with the last items from my grandmother's house, including the dolls and even three mannequins wearing costumes she'd worn in the early seventies, swathed in clear plastic but still seeping trickles of glitter.

"Careful," I called to the movers. "Those are valuable."

"Selling it all?" Eterno asked. He'd brought me coffee, black, from a nearby shop, and we stood there watching the movers and sipping from the cups.

"Most of it," I said. "But I'm buying my own place, over on Devore, so I'm keeping a few things."

"Staying in the area, eh? Good, good." His lip quirked up.

I watched the movers seal up the truck. Two of the mannequins were going to the museum of magic. The third was sticking with me, because under the sequined dress and some carefully arranged paper-mache was the automaton, with Susan's ghost still in it.

She'd agreed that some time inhabiting that shell might be a reasonable recompense for the time my grandmother had stolen from her. And she'd even indicated that she was looking forward to sharing quarters with me and investigating this strange new world, seizing the glitter, as my grandmother might have said.

How I felt about that, I wasn't entirely sure, but I was

reconciling myself to it, along with the idea that I was keeping enough stuff to furnish my own apartment.

Keeping bits that reminded me of childhood, like the comforter. History of my own, not my mother's or grandmother's. They'd stay with me, those two, and I'd always feel sorrow at their absence, but not regret. Never regret.

You can seize the glitter, but your hands have to be open, not holding onto things. Reaching forward.

Carpe glitter, my grandmother used to say. And that was what I meant to do.

About The Author

Nebula, World Fantasy, and Endeavour award nominee Cat Rambo's published work includes 200+ stories, two novels, five collections, a cookbook, a travel guide, and two books for writers, *Moving from Idea to Draft* and *Creating an Online Presence for Writers.* She runs The Rambo Academy for Wayward Writers, which offers live and on-demand online writing classes aimed at speculative fiction writers. She is a two-term President of the The Science Fiction & Fantasy Writers of America. Her 2020 publications include two novels: *Exiles of Tabat* (Wordfire Press) and *You Sexy Thing* (Tor/Macmillan). Find links and more information at www.kittyrumpus.net

Author photo © OnFocus Photography